SHAKESPEARE RETOLD

HAMLET

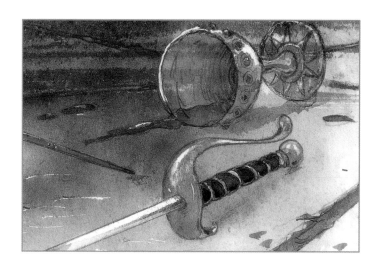

by
Martin Waddell & Alan Marks

W
FRANKLIN WATTS
LONDON•SYDNEY

First published in 2009
by Franklin Watts
338 Euston Road
London NW1 3BH

Franklin Watts Australia
45–51 Huntley Street
Alexandria
NSW 2015

Text copyright © Martin Waddell 2009
Illustrations copyright © Alan Marks 2009

Editor: Jackie Hamley
Designer: Peter Scoulding
Series Advisor: Dr Catherine Alexander of the
Shakespeare Institute, University of Birmingham

A CIP catalogue record for this book is available
from the British Library.

ISBN: 978 0 7496 7746 6 (hbk)
ISBN: 978 0 7496 7751 0 (pbk)

Printed in China

Franklin Watts is a division of
Hachette Children's Books,
an Hachette UK company.
www.hachette.co.uk

CONTENTS

THE CAST

Hamlet – Prince of Denmark
The ghost of Hamlet's father – the late king
King Claudius – Hamlet's uncle
Queen Gertrude – Hamlet's mother,
now wife of Claudius

Polonius – a lord
Laertes – son of Polonius
Ophelia – daughter of Polonius

Horatio – friend of Prince Hamlet

The castle guards, courtiers,
actors and gravediggers,
but not, alas, poor Yorick

PROLOGUE

A king's ghost cries for revenge while his murderer sits on the throne. Words cut a queen like daggers as an old man dies. His daughter, her love betrayed, drowns in a stream. A poisoned cup drips death upon a bloodstained floor.

There are deaths, too many deaths … when Hamlet, Prince of Denmark, returns to Elsinore.

CHAPTER ONE

SOMETHING ROTTEN

Hamlet, Prince of Denmark, had returned home from Germany. His father had died suddenly, and his mother, Queen Gertrude, had already married the new king, his uncle Claudius. Their hasty marriage horrified the prince. How could his mother marry so soon when she should have been mourning his father?

Now the castle guards told Hamlet that a sad
ghost stalked the walls of Elsinore. The ghost
wore battle armour and looked just like his father.

Hamlet and his friend Horatio came to the
battlements to see the ghost for themselves.

The castle beneath them echoed with the
sounds of drunken laughter, and Hamlet
felt that no one shared his grief.

"It comes, my lord!" whispered Horatio.
The ghost beckoned to the prince, and
Hamlet followed it, alone.

The ghost raised its visor, and the prince
saw his dead father's pale face.

9

"They said I was poisoned by a snake as I slept in my garden," the ghost sighed sadly. "Not so! The serpent that killed me now sits upon my throne."

"My uncle Claudius!" Hamlet groaned in despair.

"If you are a man you will avenge my death. But leave your mother to the judgement of Heaven!" implored the ghost.

"Remember me!" it said, fading away.

Hamlet rejoined Horatio. "There are more things in heaven and earth than you dream of," Hamlet told his friend.

CHAPTER TWO

A LOVE
BETRAYED

Had it really been his father's ghost or was it
an evil spirit sent to trick the young prince?

His mind in turmoil, Hamlet warned
Horatio not to speak of what he had
seen and heard, and not to be
surprised by anything that he
might do in the days to come.
The prince trusted Horatio,
but who else could
he trust?

Certainly not his uncle
or the queen, *if* the
ghost had spoken
the truth.

Even Ophelia, the girl he loved, was the
daughter of an important court official …
what if her father was using her to
discover if Hamlet suspected anything?
What if she didn't love him at all?

Hamlet had to know whether the ghost
had spoken the truth or not.

In the days that followed, Hamlet changed so much that the courtiers believed he had gone mad. The prince had been a brave and cheerful young man, but now he wandered the castle, half dressed, unwashed and talking in riddles. Ophelia's father, Polonius, watched the prince carefully.

"Hamlet talks to you of love," he warned his daughter. "But you must know he cannot marry you. A prince must make a royal marriage. Have nothing more to do with him!"

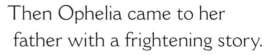

Then Ophelia came to her
father with a frightening story.

"Hamlet came to my room,"
Ophelia told Polonius.
"He grabbed my wrist.
He seemed wild with grief,
gazing at me for a long
time. Then he left
without speaking."

"The prince has lost his
reason because my
daughter has refused his
love," Polonius thought.

He went straight to the king
and queen, anxious to protect his own position at
court, and his daughter. If the prince had been
driven mad by Ophelia's refusal of his love, she
should not be blamed. She had obeyed her father,
nothing more.

"Is love the cause of Hamlet's madness?"
King Claudius wondered to himself.
"Or does he suspect me?"

"I'll test him and his love, my lord!"
Polonius told the king.

"Do you know me, my lord?" Polonius asked,
the next time he came upon the prince.

"You are a fishmonger," Hamlet sniffed,
pretending to hold his nose.

"I am not, my lord!"
gasped Polonius.

"Then I wish you were so honest a man," Hamlet replied coldly. "Tell me, fishmonger, do you have a daughter?"

"Yes, my lord," said a puzzled Polonius.

"Take care of her!" Hamlet warned. "Who knows what could happen to her?"

Was it a threat? The old courtier went to his daughter.

"Hamlet must come upon you as though by chance," he told Ophelia. "The king will hide nearby, so that he can hear what Hamlet says to you, proving your innocence."

The prince wandered alone in the Great Hall, knowing nothing of Polonius' plotting, or the presence of the king.

"To be or not to be?" Hamlet asked himself. Was it better to take a stand against his troubles and end them, or to do nothing and try to live with his conscience? To die himself would be one answer, but he feared the dreams the sleep of death might bring if he did not set things right.

"How are you my lord?" Ophelia asked softly, interrupting his thoughts. "I have gifts that I must return to you."

Hamlet no longer trusted Ophelia. His mother had betrayed his father. No woman could be trusted.

"I said I loved you, once," Hamlet mused.

"And I believed you," Ophelia replied.

"I loved you not!" Hamlet swore. "If you must marry, marry a fool, not me!" He left, muttering, "Those that are married already, all but one, shall live."

"I was right! Hamlet suspects me!" Claudius thought in his hiding place.

"It is losing my daughter's love that hurts Hamlet!" Polonius insisted.

"He doesn't look lovesick to me!" the king said.

Polonius came up with a suggestion. "Let the prince meet with the queen privately tonight. I'll hide, and tell you what they say. If his mother can't ease his mind, then send him to England, or keep him locked up somewhere safe, whichever your majesty pleases."

CHAPTER THREE

THE PLAY'S THE THING

A play was to be performed in the Great Hall.

"The king hopes this play will calm me down,"
Hamlet told Horatio as they took their seats.
"But I have worked with the actors and changed
the plot. Now it tells of the death of Duke
Gonzago, poisoned in his garden like my
father. If the king is guilty, guilt will show in
his face. The play's the thing to catch the
conscience of the king."

The play had
scarcely begun,
when ...

"Stop!" Claudius roared, storming out of the hall.
Hamlet had seen enough to confirm his
suspicions, and so had Horatio.

Claudius arranged for the prince's immediate departure to England, where he would be murdered. The men sent to guard him on the journey were given a sealed letter ordering Hamlet's death.

That done, the king found himself alone. Tortured by guilt, he knelt to pray. He did not know that Hamlet had followed him, convinced that the ghost had spoken the truth.

"I could end this now," Hamlet thought, touching his dagger. "But if I kill him while he's praying his soul will go to Heaven, when he should roast in hell! I'll find a better opportunity to kill him."

The prince hurried to his mother's room.
Polonius was already in his hiding place
there, behind a curtain.

"Leave your mother to the judgement of
Heaven … Remember me!" burned in
Hamlet's mind.

The ghost had forbidden him to harm the queen,
but she deserved punishment. He would use
words like daggers to cut her.

"Your father is offended,"
Gertrude said.

"Claudius is not my
father!" Hamlet raged.
"You betrayed my father.
How could you marry so
soon after my father's
death?" He held the queen
with her face against a
mirror, shaking her roughly.

"What do you see?" Hamlet asked bitterly.

The queen cried for help and a curtain stirred,
as someone concealed behind it moved.

"Claudius!" Hamlet thought.

He grabbed his sword and thrust it into
the body behind the curtain, again and again.

"What bloody deed have you done?"
cried the queen.

"As bloody a deed as to kill a king and
marry his brother!" Hamlet said, pulling
the curtain aside.

The body of Polonius lay bleeding
before him.

"Remember me ..." The ghost appeared again, as though to protect Gertrude from her son.

"Look!" Hamlet gasped, pointing.
"My father's there."

"No one is there," the queen wept, convinced of her son's madness.

The ghost faded away.

CHAPTER FOUR

LOVE DIES

Gertrude ran to her husband Claudius to plead mercy for her son.

"Polonius will be buried quietly, and no one will ask questions. I'll send Hamlet to England," the king consoled her.

"And Hamlet will die!" the king thought to himself.

Claudius had arranged passage for that very night, so the prince left immediately.

But Hamlet saw through the king's plan. He managed to get hold of the sealed letter, and read it.

Finally understanding the plot against him, Hamlet swapped the letter for another, ordering that the men sent to guard him should die instead. He resealed the letter with his royal seal, so that no one would suspect it had been tampered with. Then the prince made his escape.

He wrote telling Claudius that he was on his way back to Elsinore. Hamlet's letter reached the king as he faced another young man accusing him of murder.

Rumours about the death of Polonius had reached his son, Laertes. Men told of a secret burial and a trail of guilt that led to Claudius.

"My father must have been killed by you, or on your orders!" Laertes accused.

Claudius saw a neat solution to his problem: setting
Laertes against Hamlet. "Your enemy is mine,"
he convinced the young man. "Hamlet killed your
father. I had to conceal the murder to protect the
queen and Denmark."

"I'll cut his throat!" raged Laertes.

"Then I'd have to try you for his murder!" Claudius
warned. "But you will have your revenge. I'll
arrange a fencing match. He knows your reputation
as a swordsman and is too proud to refuse. You'll
both fight, but your sword will have no safety tip."

"I'll poison the blade," Laertes swore. "But Hamlet is a great swordsman. What if I cannot cut him?"

"The room will be hot. He'll sweat," Claudius smiled. "I'll hand the prince a poisoned cup to drink from. Either way, Hamlet dies."

As one death was planned, news came of another. Ophelia was found drowned in a stream, with flowers floating round her.

Some said she'd killed herself, insane with grief, but no one knew for sure.

CHAPTER FIVE

POISON FLOWS

Hamlet returned to Elsinore just as Ophelia's funeral procession entered the graveyard.

Hamlet picked up a skull from the
mound of earth and bone the
gravediggers had left.

"That skull belonged to
Yorick, your late father's
jester," he was told.

"Alas, poor Yorick, I knew him,"
Hamlet muttered. He had come to
bring death to a man he despised, and
now he held the skull of a man he had admired.

The mourners gathered round the grave.
 Laertes was arguing with the priest.

"If your sister took her own life, she should
not be buried in holy ground!" the priest insisted.
"But for the king's orders, I could not allow it."

"Ophelia will be an angel,
while you rot in hell!"
Laertes swore.

"Ophelia!" Hamlet cried, only now realising who had died.

"The devil take your soul Hamlet!" Laertes shouted, catching sight of the prince.

The two young men struggled in the open grave, until the courtiers managed to pull them apart.

"I loved Ophelia more than any brother!" Hamlet wept.

"Gertrude! Watch over your son!" the king ordered, hurrying Ophelia's brother from the graveyard.

"Have patience!" Claudius warned Laertes, reminding him of what they had decided.

It did not take long for the king to arrange the fencing match between the two young men.

"I'll bet six good horses against six French swords that Hamlet will win!" he told everyone.

The courtiers gathered in the Great Hall
to watch the two men select their weapons.
Light fencing swords called foils were brought
before them.

As they chose their foils, Hamlet begged Laertes'
forgiveness for the way he had behaved in the
graveyard. "It was my grief that caused such
madness," he said.

Leartes smiled as he picked up the
poisoned foil.

Hamlet scored the first hit. The king lifted a cup to toast Hamlet's success, and drank. Then he held up a pearl.

"This pearl is for you, Hamlet!" he said, dropping the pearl into the cup. No one saw him add poison with it, and everyone had seen him drink, so poison would not be suspected.

"Drink!" Claudius told Hamlet, handing the cup to the prince.

"Not yet!" Hamlet panted, putting the cup down.

They fought again, and Hamlet scored another hit.

The queen came forward and took the poisoned cup. "A toast to my son!" she said, raising it to her lips.

"Don't drink!" the king hissed, but his warning came too late.

"Once more, Laertes?" Hamlet asked, raising his foil.

This time, Laertes fought fiercely, and grazed the prince with the poisoned foil.

Blood flowed, and both men dropped their weapons.

Hamlet reached down for his foil ... but he picked up Laertes' poisoned one instead, without realising his mistake.

Hamlet mortally wounded his rival.

"Hamlet!" groaned the dying Laertes. "The foil was poisoned. We were both cut by it. We both will die. Look to the queen. She dies too. She drank from a poisoned cup Claudius meant for you. The king's to blame for all our deaths!"

"Murderer!" roared the prince, running the king through. With the last of his strength, he forced the poisoned cup to his uncle's lips. "Drink ... and follow my mother to the grave!"

The prince fell, the poison pounding in his veins.

"Goodnight, sweet prince," Horatio said softly,
as Hamlet died.

Epilogue

Claudius, the queen, Polonius,
Laertes, Ophelia and the prince ...

There were deaths, too many deaths ...
when Hamlet, Prince of Denmark,
returned to Elsinore.

NOTES

by Dr Catherine Alexander

Hamlet is a ghost story, a murder mystery,
a family tragedy, and a political saga.
But above all, it is a play about a young man,
Prince Hamlet, with a major moral problem:
Is it ever right for someone to take the law into
his own hands? Is it ever right to kill a person?

So the play explores the rights and wrongs of
taking revenge: of breaking the law (both the
law of the land and God's law) to achieve justice
and to solve a problem that the law can't or
won't deal with.

The old king (Hamlet's father) has been
murdered by his brother Claudius. Claudius is
now king of Denmark and has married Hamlet's
mother Gertrude. What should Hamlet do?
What can he do? Should he believe the ghost?
Can he trust his mother? Can he trust his

friends? Can he trust Ophelia? How can he challenge a king?

This moral complexity and the hero's dilemma have made *Hamlet* one of the most famous plays in the world, and the language of the play is as memorable as the plot.

Hamlet thinks about his problems in his famous soliloquies. These are the speeches that he speaks out loud when he is alone on stage, sharing his thoughts with the audience. These soliloquies contain some of Shakespeare's best known lines, most famously, "To be or not to be …"

Shakespeare's friend, the leading actor Richard Burbage, was probably the first man to play Hamlet when the play was written around 1600. Legend has it that Shakespeare himself – and he was an actor as well as a playwright – played the part of the ghost so the two friends might have performed together on the stage of the Globe theatre. When Shakespeare died in 1616 he left Burbage money in his will to buy a ring.

A mystery surrounds the text of *Hamlet*. For many years it was known that there were two slightly different versions of the play – the one published in a single volume during Shakespeare's lifetime (1604) and the one published in the book known as the First Folio, the collection of his plays that was published by his friends after his death.

In 1823 a different version was rediscovered in the British Library in London. This is only half the length of the others and had been published earlier than them, in 1603. Some thought that this must have been Shakespeare's first draft of the play but scholars have now decided that this shorter *Hamlet* was recreated by an actor who had performed in the longer play and then tried to make money by getting it published before the others. He was able to remember the plot but obviously couldn't remember everyone's lines.

HAMLET FACTS

❖ The part of Hamlet has been performed in many ways over the last four hundred years: he has been played on stage as an action hero, a romantic lead, a philosopher and a madman. David Garrick, the great eighteenth-century actor, thrilled audiences as Hamlet when he saw his father's ghost. He had a special attachment to his wig and could pull a string to make his hair stand on end in fright.

❖   The play has been performed all over the world, sometimes with a female actor playing the prince.

❖   *Hamlet* has a long history in film. At the end of the nineteenth century, the great French actress Sarah Bernhardt played Hamlet (in French). The duel scene from that production was filmed in France in 1900. An early silent film was a German production of the play with the Danish actress Asta Nielsen in the title role.

❖   Probably the best known *Hamlet* films are those directed by and starring Sir Lawrence Olivier (1948) and Kenneth Branagh (1997). Both men had had great success performing the role on stage.